C000212263

THE QUANTUM
PILGRIMAGE:

An Existential Quest to the

Quantum Self

By Isaac R. Betanzos

Front & back covers by Zdzisław Beksiński

Cover & Online edit by Andrew Tabash

All illustrations sourced from wikimedia.org

ISBN: 9781087237824

For an enhanced introspection, read it in a quiet place with background instrumental music.

"To those embracing and pursuing the abstract essence of existence."

TABLE OF CONTENTS

Zdzisław Beksiński. Sanok Museum

<u>PROLOGUE</u>

In certain key existential conjunctions we encounter, the only way to find your true nature as being is by losing everything first; by skinning your bare soul until it's down to its narrow essence; by giving up all that you assume 'being you' involves. It is then, when you dislodge yourself from all the biological roar and clamour, when the thunderous clarity will hammer your reality. Because to admire the inherited nature of a rainbow, you must first undress it from all its deceiving colours.

Expect the unexpected, disbelieve in the goal, fear the wish, cherish the journey. Wisdom and transcendence are not awaiting at the end of that tortuous and devious passage; but guilefully veiling in the crevices within your soul and the trail itself.

As an answer can only be found after formulating the right question; and, then, be ready to tremble and crumb in the presence of that sought truth. Each stroll will only make your quest harder; but for everything worth a memory, and for everything left behind after we perish, effortless is not in range.

Time is just the wind carrying whispers: from the past to our survival-obsessed brain; from the future to our deaf higher-self mind. The present is the solid voice balancing in that thin and shaking thin rope. It is down to our basic and intrinsic self-conviction to discern between both, and whisper back as an echo that re-defines the established status-quo.

Space is the trap and illusion that cages our instinctive nature, guarded by our bodies and biological limitations. Courage and awareness are the key to bend and slip through our mental jail bars. Because for the aspects of existence that truly matter, distance is not a question of physical separation, but of spiritual affiliation and languageless understanding.

As the moment you truly figure out the angle where you stand within your network of meaningful connections, it is also the instant where you no longer have sight of the reality being unfolded in front of you.

Because it is only when you are ultimately and deeply lost, when you will be gifted with the opportunity to redefine everything you are to this world, in a moment of pure conviction. Allow terror

7

and demons to own you, so that you can dazzle them with the shine gleamed from your bravery and determination.

Ignite and revere that brightness no matter the consequences, as it is the only reverie separating us from ultimate darkness...

Zdzisław Beksiński. Sanok Museum

PHASE 1: Ascension

The blinding warm light penetrates through my eyelids, driving a feeling of unstoppable fulfilment across my veins. Suddenly, the space and matter that confine my body expand to make enough room for the flowing of my overwhelming and blooming energy. Finally, my eyes open. In front of me, the paradise irradiated from my soul unfolds. For an impetuous moment, the sunlight, yellow and magnanimous, collapses my senses until all the colours of reality find their place one by one.

I am both above and below, and everything that it was, is or will be. I float governed by my own will, overseeing everything that is beautiful and worth existing for. Up there, at my back, an open blue sky full of possibilities and promises. Down there, under me, a multisensory and endless field, where each one of the pigments and shades transpire all the positive sentiments ever conceived. Where I am now, time is just the wind snuggling me as I drift through it, moving it forwards and backwards with no set destination or purpose: I am the impenetrable castle of my own kingdom.

The green grass and the infinite flowers welcome me with grace as I overfly them. They grant me with their crisp smell transported by the breeze and charged with bracing humidity. The sound becomes a sweet and soft frolic merriment to me, shaped at my will like if I was engraving the everlasting grandeur envolving me. With a gesture from my hand, the fulfilled and reassuring Sun in front of me responds to my wishes, coordinating the multidimensional orchestra I'm witnessing.

There is everything I need in here, since I no longer need anything at all. In the horizon, I perceive and master the forest, trees and every single leaf or strand of glass; the clouds dance to the rhythm of my own thoughts; each colour is impregnated with the scent of a promise to grow and reach newgrounds; the silence is filled with a solemn melody that bends with the landscape, blurring the frontier between the sky and the mountains, too far away to stand confrontation with the projection of their shadow.

There is too much gleeful light and beauty tamed by my yearning to allow anything to be impossible in my realm… As I fly in that powerful and magnificent eternity, the boundaries of my body, mind and soul weld together, forgiving their confines. I am both individuality restrained within and a plurality flourished from my ecosystem.

And, up there, far beyond everything that is known or devised, a star emerges: the brightest star the sky has ever hosted. I am blinded by its beauty and the promise of splendor. My whole kingdom becomes magnetised by that solitaire, unique, shimmering star in the distant amplitude. Suddenly, the entire world unveiled in front of me points towards that secluded and endless brightness, calling me on everything I am as a being. Everything that is beautiful and worth down here must be shared with that yonder blaze up there. Suddenly, my human condition becomes corporeal again, embracing me into a quest to pursuit the allure that announces a new reality. No matter the price required, this bond and urge that I feel inside is unbreakable.

I fly higher, faster, sharper while tunnelling all my contained beauty and power towards the promised eternal exhilaration by my star. It is the motorway of my fate from which I choose not to scape. I stretch my arm, hand and fingers, eager to reach that star isolated in the eternal sky: for an instant I'm getting so close that I can scent a whole new palette of colours approaching; everything that I have experienced up until then feels grey and superfluous.

For just an imperishable moment, I am connected to that wildly tamed star with an invisible strength that defies all logic: for an invaluable moment, I am the star and the star is I. And everything becomes purposeful. As we redefine together all the wisdom of existence, she whispers me the major truth of reality that there is: words that shall forever be adhered to my soul with recurring twinge and laceration.

All the sudden, my legs start to weight. The ground, far underneath, calls and demands me for trial because of my audacity. As I begin to fall, the clouds gather and start to conspire against me, interrupting the sight with my star: they will be the accusation witnesses during my trial. However, as fools they fail to insulate us apart, as the moment we shared was woeful and transcended the physical futilities of reality or perception.

The Sun, now engulfed with an impetuous red colour and filled with a silent rage of disbelief for my daring, raises back up as the solemn judge of this nonsense. I fall swiftly and undoubtedly to the ground, where a multicolour jury will dictate my fate. Everything that once belonged to the kingdom of my own will has rebelled against me as the necessary price to pay to thrive towards real delight and purpose.

I hit the ground hard, deafening all my senses, and the slap of the mundane and physical reality tastes like a nightmare from which I cannot find the way out. My hands try to grip to all the colours and strands of green grass to desperately hold onto any kind of comfort. Instead, realism wins another battle against my mind, showing me that it was just brown and pestilent mud down here all along. No further trace of the flowers and infinite colours that I confounded myself with. As I lean on my knees, they plunge deep and cold in the sludge, penetrating every pore of my skin and spirit. I try to scream, but no sound comes out of my throat; my ears sharpen to discern the whispers carried by my old ally the wind: they have turned into ceaseless echoes that torment my overwhelmed soul, replicating the ravaging reality disclosed.

Everything is brown, wet and fickle from where I stand, and as I am swallowed by the muck, I also lose control and will over my body and confused mind. I am a fatality of the very same reality that I created. No colours, no music and no scent of the beauty I had foreseen from above: just a nauseous bog around me covering me up to the neck. From that cruel pit of reality, all I can willingly do now is to raise my eyes up to witness what's left of my star, behind those rowdy clouds, one last time. And as I renounce to ever endure such pureness

18

again, the sky cries out my verdict: the Sun gives up to the blood Moon and welcomes the darkness of the most lonesome night.

The clouds cheer and clap with boisterous thunders learning my final destiny, still jealous of my love and endowment towards the compassionate beauty of my star. They become the warders of my existence, tempering abiding gravity as the cell to contemplate the cost of my defiance for eternity. Then, a drop falls down my forehead and into my mouth: it has the pungent taste of revenge and the weight of all the hues in the world that I have now lost. A million more follow in a turbulent gust, as the drizzle comes closer as a misty fog to mock my complacent misfortune.

Surrender by the tempest, rotting mud, darkness and thicke smog, my soul fades away capitulating my sanity to this callous reality to which I am the crafter. The wind rebels and strengthen, fed by my own weakness and throes, slapping me, carrying the ever-painful last revelations from that star that I touched once. Each murmur trespasses my crust like a puny thorn that finds its way to the core of my pain, where my soul is most vulnerable and volatile.

Everything that once was beautiful and eternal is now terrestrial, hefty and claustrophobic. The water, the mud and the sorrow will soon cover everything that I have ever embraced and believed in, summing me into its eternal night...

As I glance up at the sky, remembering my escapement and mastering of everything that was, is and will be, I gasp that mesmerising and stunning star one last time, still shyly shining across the clouds. For a moment, I can recall and feel the overwhelming warmth that I clustered within my fingertips for a minimal instant: for that last time, I recall all the essence of colours tastes and sounds from everything that is worthful in this world, encouraged by my star standing still and tall in the sky. So close to what's left of my heart up there, and so far from everything that I am now.

As I get ready to accept and embrace this obscurity, the breeze brings me its last derision, rejoicing in my absolute defeat: "was it worth it, you fool?"

And as those words penetrate my rachitic soul, the last spark of sense left untouched in me rages with the glow of a dying and insurgent flame, carving my obituary into the eternity of my self-created, perfect and collapsing world: "it is better to have witnessed and fought for the empowering and alluring everlasting beauty of an unreachable star, than contenting yourself with the emptiness and deceiving reality of the shallow deed. If everything that I am is the price to pay to embosom such grandiose instant of achievement and connection, all I ask for is for another chance to do exactly the same again..."

I don't know how much longer I will last; the dusk and blackness is now kissing my eyes with a enrapture stupefy... And my soul is ready to give up to that gentle good night...

Moonlit Landscape by C. Carus. Dresden Art

<u>PHASE 2: Decampment</u>

The blinding cold darkness penetrates through my eyelids, driving a feeling of unstoppable disintegration across my veins. Suddenly, the space and matter that confines my body shrinks and shakes to contain the draining of my leaking energy. Finally, my eyes open. In front of me, the obscurity created by my soul unfolds. For an impetuous moment, the moonlight cries bitter blood, until the shades gather and find their place one by one.

I am lying in the ground, mud dripping all around my back, where the air I am breathing can be cut with a blade of sorrow. Up there, the clouds still gather together rejoicing my fatal fall, throwing pity and judgement at me in the form of stiff and corrosive drops. My

Sunset Star hides behind them, somewhere up there, and with gargantuan agony, I come to understand that I will never be in her presence again. Yet somehow, I can still embrace myself with her infinite light, resembling as a fresh memory of eternal light.

The wind brings the putrid smell of the ruins from my bold audacity. It also whispers at me, reminding me that solemn instant when I connected with the highest level of myself, when I wasn't a slave of my own desire. The breeze also dictates that I shall never speak her name again, and that pretending she was never there will save me from insanity: but my mind is already overflowed with a memoir I refuse to forget. Even dwelling in that pain feels sweeter than the emptiness of the silence encompassing me.

Surrender by a vast empire of nothingness, time clicks, one second at the time, impassive to my anguish. As this gale is now lineal, predictably unpredictable, and a burden to make me accountable for everything I have lost. Space chooses to become my antagonist, impetuous and wild, it rebels around me filling the terrain with barriers to test whatever is left of me. A part of me knows I need to fly higher than ever, spending eternity searching for reunion with my Sunset Star if obliged; my reality pledges for uncontested surrender in the form of an increasing gravity.

As my throat stays mute, somewhere in that field of anguish, a distant snarl raises. The slush which had me prisoner suddenly spits me out with fear and nervousness. The wind flutter more vivaciously and with a sense of uneasiness. Even the clouds up there stop their grotesque celebration and await with expectation. The moon stops bleeding and hides, adding blackness to my world. As the roaring rumbles stronger and closer, it becomes clear to me: the Monster, my final executioner, is coming to retrieve and inhale the scraps of what's left of me.

As I recline in the ground, taciturn to my destiny while everything around me rattle with uncertainty, my doom almost feels like mercy. I close my eyes with serenity, accepting the price tag requested for that unbreakable moment of real happiness. What is left of me is no longer worth the run away for my survival. However, as I lie down with tranquillity, I suddenly feel some warmth coming from within: a tiny segment from my Sunset Star, which was impregnated into me when we fondled each other to our core.

Then, abrupt revolution. The Monster pleas and claims the last beautiful particle left in this negligent world that I have forged. Fear penetrates every pore of my essence, acknowledging that I cannot oblige and give up the last bit of light from my Sunset Star that remains in me. Because the very same last memory of her that haunts me down at every single breath, is the one that also enables that breathing. She has turned into my gift and my curse concurrently.

I must protect and preserve that sparkle of delicacy that makes existence meaningful; I must hide it away from this impetuous and restless beast. My legs, now that my wings have been slaughtered, finally decide to respond to my command to commence my desperate getaway. Where to go when all lights have vaporised and you are made of the same darkness you are attempting to smuggle from?

There is no time for contemplation, the Monster is narrowing, and I can already smell its fetid and noxious odour from where I stand. And that growling… that grunting is made with the texture endless nightmares are formed. The air becomes opaquer, burdensome and stifling as its presence turns suffocating, while decimating everything that is left around with repentance.

I run, I run like if my legs were eternally unsatisfied with the broad distance they can cover with each stride. However, the dense and sinister forest lying in the horizon to provide me with despondent shelter seems to spurt faster from me. In addition, with every breath, I capitulate another flake from my broken spirit. Nevertheless, my last mission is to protect the last strand of light in this world.

I fall repeatedly for a trillion million times, and with each collapse the remembrance of my Sunset Star encourages me to raise tall again and continue my last quest. I am too startled to look back and face the Monster; at the same time, that moment of glory when the star and I were indivisible, draws bittersweet tears down my face, signing stories of extinguishing happiness. A part of me stayed in that bright blue sky anchored into the past; another part, never contrived to stand up from the mud during the judgement day; the rest of me, waivers on capitulating. I crawl as if if I were hiking the tallest and sharpest of mountains, yet the path in front of me is flat. Just stand up one more time, the gloomy forest does not seem that far away now.

As I finally reach that murky thicket, I spot a twisted path on my right. When I resolve to jaunt it, a minuscule twinkle emerges before my eyes. Like an oasis of blaze in the middle of the blackest night, this Enchanter claims my attention: with decisive gestures of elation, it appeals to whatever compassion is left in me to trail her down this passage. Temptation to fall for that pledge of redemption feels like if intent streamed my life again. However, too convenient to be true, I grasp that it is no more than just a gimmick from the Monster to slow me down with false promises of relief.

Puckering my gesture, I present my back to the Enchanter and opt to bend myself with the density of the dusk of that forest, filled with wistful. I must remain focused and tunnelled towards my quest of preserving the last fragment contained within myself that has any value. As the sparkle of the Enchanter vanishes behind, I surprisingly start to feel more accommodated within the mourning that conforms my existence and everything that is pernicious around me.

I dig deeper and deeper inside the forest. I create trails where there was only remorse and contrition. I cannot tell if I have been running away for minutes, hours or centuries; where I am now is too deep into the realm of existence to discern the volatilities of time and space. I survive drinking and rejoicing myself with the echoes from my past, dripping through the scars carved by the extinction of my being.

There is no rest, there is no sleep. Just drunken accumulation of moments one after the other, fighting to stay one step ahead of that restless Monster that is chasing me, picking up the trail sketched by my weakness. No matter how much I advance, I always come back to that path on the edge between this endless forest and the valley of nothingness. And no matter how many times I find myself in that same berth, I never cull for the pathway the Enchanter advocated.

All that exists around me is cold and inert, aiming to grab and strip me from the remains of my grace. To find flames and colours I must look within and retrace the beautiful moments that bind me with my Sunset Star. No matter what is required of me, I will not let the Monster cop the last essence of magnificence in this world. No matter how much is breaking me down, I will never stop recalling what deemed my happiest juncture.

However, as I run in circles for eternity, finally my spirit reaches the deepest of grottos of existence: I find myself at the feet of the tallest mountain. Entombed by its glooming obscurity, I am both on the verge of my freedom and trapped between a wall of impossibilities and that pestilent Monster. I barely have the strength to stand in my feet, but the cruel destiny is compelling me for one last act of heroism and climb where no one has ever been before. The titanic task might end what's left of me.

While I ponder and size up the amount of vitality left in me, that voice carried by the wind mocks and challenges me once more: "will it be worth it, you twit?"

And as those words sink in my decrepit soul, the last spark of purity left untouched in me revolts my eternal dictum, bringing once more words sculpted by the remnants of my heart: "because this world is filled with staggering darkness and sorrow, holding up to the last vestiges of luster exonerates such a meaningful crusade. Because of my sins and misdeeds, it will…"

However, I must hurry to preserve my Sunset Star, because the joy she gifted me with is ephemeral as are the detritus of my own existence…

Isaac R. Betanzos / *The Quantum Pilgrimage*

The Dark Mountain by M. Hartley. Metropolitan Art Museum

PHASE 3: Escalation

I contemplate the soaring and unconquerable mountain from the deepest of my pit for an ephemeral eternity. As my lungs desperately beseech for a grasp of air and a reason to not falter at the feet of the colossus, the rumble peals impetuous from the dismal trees at my back. The Monster is not conceding in his snaring for what's left of my soul; that behemoth will find no rest until it seizes the remaining luster of my Sunset Star.

Where I find no reasons to pursuit, I also encounter no possibility to halt. As for whatever is worthful and left in me, this peak severs me from my ultimate intent. While the Moon refuses to offer me any kind of shelter in the shape of leading brightness, I must hold onto the obscurity to guide me in what my next leap should be. However, one can find no answers unless the questions are formulated with an aimed purpose.

I do not ask for forgiveness, as the sentence feels light for the crime. I do not dwell in grim as I once connected with the purpose of life. I accept my overdose of mundane dust and clay as for a flash I was the sky and the sky was I. I shall not go willingly or effortless, as I now detain in my heart the last slice that holds this world together. Keep roaring you unruly beast, while there is a whiff left in my spirit, there is the unbreakable eagerness to continue losing this war.

My hands clench to the steep tall wall, and almost motionless they start to search for the next higher ground, in an endless traipse. My feet twist and shrink with the putrid smell of the Monster that is almost touching them as they raise up high away from its starved jaws. Suddenly, the time transported by the breeze decides to relentless play with my wit: as everything remains obscure, the days and eons come back and forth, dancing with the residues of my self-control.

I hike above the forest skyline and allow my raw and fatigued soul to inspire that instant of peace, glimpsing the leftovers of my kingdom. For everything that was once colourful, joyful and buoyant it is now shady, morose and disabused instead. Not even an inkling of the beauty that ruled that open and immense sky, but just closeness and resentment to the person I dared to be.

I must continue climbing this thankless trail, filled with grind and volatility, while I hear the piercing wail of the Monster pleading for my final fail. Even in my attempted sleep, I find myself in this tiny room cloistered with my memories, my drubbings and that humongous beast that reminds me everything I have lost even before I had anything. Moreover, as my eyes come to life, reality mocks me while I yearn to go back to my trance ordeal.

I am ascending in my quest, yet with every stride I find myself a bit deeper within my bleakness. Wanders of the meaning of existence and the reasons for continuance strike my head like a hedge hammer abusing a compassionate and solitaire strand of grass. However, where I come from and where I am going to have no room for contemplation and self-reflection: I must continue my suicidal expedition towards redemption.

The ridge decides to scorn against me, while stretching higher in a serpentine foreshortening that averts me from my duty. And with every new contour in my path, I find new reasons that bring me back to that instance when I had everything just long enough to lose it all. And for that boundless moment of agony, an instant to taste bliss is encapsulated and smuggled.

After that eternity of frustration and vexation, I quell the ground that marks the cap of that cruel peak. As I accommodate in that bleak ground, the rocks dance and prickle my body deprecating my feat. Just as every element within and without, they revolt against my essence, nature and beliefs. Perhaps if I manage to restore the light in this doomed and fading world, I will be worthy of the vindication of my soul.

I inhale the corrupted air at the top of that hill and see nothing but the obscure oblivion; hear nothing but a silent and stinging shriek; taste nothing but my own acrimonious failure; smell nothing but the revolting texture of collapse; feel nothing but the last traces of my beautiful Sunset Star, crafted as distant memories that torment and sustain my fainted ghost.

Not even the vast immensity before me is enough to cover the height, length and weight of my regrets. Not even that vast enormity finds a corner where to shelter any strain of forgiveness. However, it does not matter, as for everything that I lost to get here was just the coarse reflection of what I formerly won: my present agony shall be just the grotesque depict of my erstwhile delight.

My restful moment decides to flee before my troubled mind attains any shard of wisdom from it. The Monster mounts and ascends with its pincers, annihilating the world I believed tore us apart. That unflagging villain seems as determined for its luminous price as I am to dissert from it. As I feel my Sunset Star anxiously waiving inside my chest with ache and soreness, I understand this evasion is far from over.

I scope my surroundings looking for answers to the questions that cannot be formulated. Suddenly, right on the opposite slope, the teeny sparkle of the Encharter comes to life. That little nymph seeks my attention once more, pointing towards an appealing way out. Right at the end of that downhill path, a modest cluster of lodges gather to welcome the lonely walker.

As the possibility of siding with civilisation raises as a luscious temptation to cram my spirit with, it almost felt like my only choice. However, too convenient to be true, I grasp that it is no more than just a gimmick from the Monster to corner and hunt me down at a closer and more comfortable range. Encouraged by my claustrophobic tunnelled view for escape, I choose to turn my back to the Enchanter and find my way across the arduous and onerous trail instead.

If that was the culmen of moments for choices, my standing shall not be found amongst equals, as my acts and experiences condemned me to toast my uniqueness with solitude. As I part, I introspect my farewells to whatever was left as civilised inside of me. It is clear now, if it ever wasn't, that there is no coming back from where I have been and towards where I am leading myself into.

As when you wassail and drown yourself in the most extreme poles within the spectrum continuum of endurance and essence, you no longer belong to this world, nor to other. Thus I can only roam on the edge of existence, like a blind funambulist that holds the weight of its past and future as the cane to keep the balance. The rod I dance in might be thin and shudder, yet my determination and fortitude will holt high and firm.

And, as the sound of loneliness and isolation aligns with the horizon and the soil under my feet, I must find the animus to solve the riddle of perseverance. As I am not allowed to give in to my sorrow and eternal rest just yet, I furl to the light and warmth inside my bosom that remind me the meaning brawling for a lost cause. As I search for my Sunset Star within myself, I find the nourishment to jump into the next stage of my journey.

Behind me, the most beautiful and haunting remembrances of everything that I was and made me purposeful are now gone forever; in front of me, a narrow and dark trail towards a desperate and quixotic salvation from my own mistakes. Even if the verdict was chanted with compunction, my soul refuses to comply and submit everything that I once stood for.

I now presumably face an eternity of penitence ahead of me. Yet I refuse to look down, left or right, back or forth: I can only look up to the sky and contemplate that magnanimous empty space that used to accommodate the most beautiful creation the firmament has ever met. Now, I must preserve what's left of *what once made me the most blessed being in creation.*

While I hasten and spurt my irreducible goal, that voice carried by the wind attempts to unbalance my determination by seeding further doubt in my agitated heart: "was that wise, you stooge?"

And as the words rumble the last pieces of me standing, I am granted with voice once more to expound my ultimate intention to this tyrannical fate: "because sometimes, in order to feel whole for a concise moment, you must be ready to surrender your nature and detach yourself from everything you know and where you no longer belong to, it was…"

When all I found reasons for was to collapse and cease to exist, that inner light irradiated from my Sunset Star illuminated the path in this endless night, pushing me to fight for her preservation once more...

Isaac R. Betanzos / *The Quantum Pilgrimage*

Zdzisław Beksiński. Sanok Museum

PHASE 4: Banishment

On the verge of the abysm, I face the riddle that shall dictate the ventures of my fate: at one side of the furrow, the promise of that distant civilisation that offers trivial comfort and predictability, demanding the surrender of the light left in me; on the opposite side of the ring, the wild uncertainty of the desert of tribulation, where I get another day to preserve what's still hued and holy in this corrupt world. Pulled by the laceration strings attached to my cracked hurt, I know my only choice is banishment and exile.

As I turn my back on everything I have ever known, cheered and created, I fall repentantly in that abysmal and unabated desert of tribulation. Every direction calk the rest, and only a seamed and enfeebled chunk of wood, resting by my feet, sparks variation in the monochromatic landscape. It does not matter which beeline I undertake, as the sand is as grey, dull and impeached in every direction.

Regardless of my feeling of being standing eons away from where I come from, the Monster never doze. My troubled senses still can smell it, and my agitated contemplation hears that roar somewhere too far away to be seen, yet too close by to lean. That gargoyle is still searching for my Sunset Star, and it will not cease until she is ripped off from the dregs of my spirit. As my last conscious intent, I shall not capitulate the wrecks of my beliefs.

I walk and stroll for a time that extends to eternity and beyond, yet nothing seems to advance. The horizon remains still, unreachable, unaltered, unprovoked. Day and night blend together in a sadistic dance that turns everything around pallid. Not even one colour to be admired and worth cheering for. I am no longer part of this reality, yet my body resists its final breath, teasing me with each heartbeat.

As I endure my useless and purposeful wander, the sand below my feet tries to trap me with each step. The steam and the heat climbs from the core of the planet itself, infecting the air and each grain of gravel with rage. Everything in the outside is hotter than the surface of the very same Sun than once obeyed me. Yet, inside the crumbs of my corpse, everything feels wintry and numbing, impeding me from clustering any meaningful sensation.

I can only differentiate drowsiness from vigil because in the former I am tortured with the images of everything I have had to give up so far. Twisted in despair, I stand in front of my missing star, but she refuses to acknowledge me anymore: she can no longer recognise the being that once flew so high just to connect with her. She has renounced from those who once sacrificed everything they were in order to become part of her shine.

As I wake up, I wish I could go back to the endless and cruel nightmare. Nothing feels more piercing and destructive than knowing I will never stand in front of her again. When I raise my eyes to the sky, the clouds gather and mimic the grey and lugubrious colours from down below. Their resentment seems to have no end, while they still judge and plume with my punishment.

If I need to find meaning and beauty in this world, I can only introspect and scratch my decrepit soul until I go deep enough. Right there, in the profound of existentialism, I shelter the sparkle. The last gift ever conceded, so fragile that it would vanish with even mentioning it. Then, for a brief moment of isolation, my memories dance to the music of how does it feel like when you feel at all.

With cherish I implore for a way out to this unfinishable routine. Stride after stride, all become a repetition of pain, loss, and heaviness to the soul. Perhaps the next one will change everything. Yet, it just serves a purpose to dig my foot under the sand, like the previous one, and like the next one promises to be. Moreover, as I have been running away for centuries, I look down: that seamed and enfeebled chunk of wood is again resting by my feet.

Thirst. Insatiable thirst burst from my innards reminding me that I am still corporeal, mortal, disposable. With nothing within sight reach to calm it, I am forced to drain and gulp my own blood in a hysterical circle of self-obliteration. Through each pore, I lick it with desperation and indignity, looking to make it a bit longer, prolonging this senseless anguish.

As the prohibited liquid returns into my body, my senses start to blurry and mix. What is sand and what belongs to me, is no longer for me to decide. Locating my spirit and my body in space has become an unusually hard challenge. My head spins and my body follows like the loyal servant towards carnage. I have lost the command over my willingness and motor functions.

As confusion reigns and steps collapse, I can hear the landscape mocking me with a despicable gallantry. I stand still, yet everything moves and revolves in a chaotic manner, turning the upside downs of my monotonous trail. I am no longer aware of whether I am moving forward or stepping directly towards the Monster's claws. For all I know, he might be eating my heart while I still pretend that I am alive. Suddenly, a lapse of clarity: my blood has been tainted and adulterated with my own guilt and remorse. I try to scream but no one will listen. Where I have arrived, I am too far gone from the reach of where any other being has been before.

Solitude. Isolated. Secluded. Silenced. Confined. Detached. Exiled. Banished.

Vanished.   Segregated.   Concealed. Expelled. Deported. Insulated. Recused. Desolated.   Outcasted.   Obscured. Abandoned. Discarded. Forsaken. Jilted. Rejected.   Relinquished.   Withdrawn. Yielded.   Waived.   Dumped.   Ditched. Vacated.   Disappeared.   Departed. Dissolved. Evaporated. Expired. Faded. Retreated.   Ceased.   Disregarded. Exterminated. Decimated. Extinguished. Obliterated. Eradicated. Slaughtered. All consequence of my retrospective choice.

Memories jump spontaneously like ephemeral bombs of sorrow all around me. They collapse in the fraction of the moment just before my eyes and right after they penetrate my senses. As a grotesque parade, they pop and fade before I can enjoy them, but right after they puncture my zest. I cannot recognise and divide my self-created reality from this punishment that repeats itself in crumbling circles.

I witness everything that made me happy once, and I witness it disappearing the moment after. Just like that, I lose everything again, and again, and again... For everything beautiful that I created and shared, it is now left behind and clustered by the impenetrable and unreachable cell of the past. From where I stand now, those cues and images summarise all my defeats and each one of them represent a lost chunk of my soul.

For a trillion times spread across a million centuries I must observe all the colours, scents, sounds, tastes and feels that I will never experience again. The entire world I had to leave behind and give up as a result of a dream that was not ready to be awaken. Like bubbles they raise, majestically fragile, then vanish and perish before me, reminding me that I killed and wasted every gift that was given to me.

Every last one, except the most profound one. As I witness that imperishable moment when I was my star and my star was I. In this closed and obscure night, I foresee with pain those fireworks that once transported me to another reality. That interdimensional trip where I discovered that the colours, shapes and forms that I had believed until then this world is made of, were just coarse scribbles of what truly bliss is fabricated with.

And for a trillion times spread across a million centuries, I am reunited with my start for an instant at the time. Then I lose her forever again, and the world becomes solitaire and meaningless once more. And this destructive night refuses to end or bring any hope. My misery and misfortune are the result of my own bravery and foulness towards pursuing all those colours I was once intoxicated with...

While I twist and cram in that eternal cycle of memoirs, the wind brings that corrupted voice again to strike me with the final push into the ulterior shallow: "Were they worth it, you pawn?"

And as the words blow all the remaining bubbles with a violent harmony, a guttural sound comes out of my throat, aware that I will never stand in front of those beautiful memories ever again: "As for everything that lives long enough to cause pain, it is just a boorish reflection of the happiness and fulfilment that also brought to your life; as for all the pain we are capable to fabricate in this reality, we were so lucky to inhale the colours that craft meaning to the Universe. Because I hurt, I once reached real joy. Because without darkness, we cannot value the light. Because renouncing to pain, is renouncing to happiness. Because I can't do that, they were worth it…"

It is time now to abandon the desert of tribulation, before my last sparkle of life decides to abandon me… It is not a question of time anymore, as time stopped back then, when I was part of the sky…

Stormy Sea with Lighthouse - C. Blechen. Bridgeman

PHASE 5: Peregrination

As I open my eyes with heaviness, I fathom that I must undertake my long journey towards the nameless; at the same time, I will be spurting my past, now revamped into both gift and curse, joy and anguish. Because the Monster still follows close by. Like a bloodhound, it traces the scent of my inner frailty, revealing that luminous trail leading to the remains of my Sunset Star inside me. And I, like a preposterous and whimsical mirror, discern its fetid and hairy whiff back.

Just like that, the inquest contra immensity begins. I leave the desert of tribulation fast paced. However, a burning and harrowing feeling strikes me from my left side, slowing my strides. As I look down to my chest, I find that seamed and enfeebled chunk of wood now resting between my ribs instead of by my feet. It nails deep, rooting and embracing my weakened heart merciless. The pain is unbearable, like a constant piercing ache that reminds me of my misery every time I breathe.

Nevertheless, I cannot take the luxury of stopping to assess my wounds. That restless miscreation is chasing me much closer than I feel comfortable with. I must find a place in this infamous world where I can lay down the last particle of beauty and move on, re-joining with what brought so much colour and sense to my existence once. As I start walking again, that wooden and rotten peg finds a way to dig deeper into my soul with each step.

Without any more resent or lachrymose, I cross the horizon in front of me over and over again, searching for that promised land of forgiveness. As I reach the edge of the desert, the perspective of that new start craves closer. I penetrate into an entire new world, one where the Sun decides to rise up in the sky again, and where the clouds no longer conspire against me.

I am surrounded by an endless grazing of withered grass. The emotionless weeds stay static and dance passively to the blow of the random wind. No sound is carried; no danger is at sight either. It would seem that there is everything a being could need to find satisfaction and fulfilment. A sterile river flows slowly and motionless on the side, like if it carried the melancholy of an old song no longer remembered.

As I continue exploring, there is no shelter to hide from the searing sunlight. Not even one tree to remember me the

69

taste of fruit or the sweetness of resting. Animal life forms left those moors long ago, probably aware of the doom that overflies this dormant empire. I find everything that is new to my world, yet it all feels so disappointingly and hauntingly familiar. There is a melody of beginning floating in the static air, even if around me I can only perceive endings.

I have everything I could need right here; yet, there is nothing here that awakens any of my senses or emotions. Just like the grass below me, I am dead inside. Because I cannot bury and withhold that sentiment of profound loss here, I know my memories will still torment me should I settle in this world. Because, across the distance, that hairy and vigorous Monster is approaching, claiming its guerdon, I must move on... And, as I pronounce that thought, I find myself again on the edge of that desert, ready to start my scouting once more.

I resume my quest towards truth, while the wooden stake waltz around my heart with disrespect. I cross the horizon over and over again, staying just ahead of my seemingly inevitable destiny. Finally, I reach shore and feel the tingle of debased water on my toes. I am at the feet of the most capacious sea that there is.

The water is drab and dusty. It moves like a fragile and slender serenade that hides the most turbulent stream under its thin surface. The impetuous wind that slaps my face at the shoreline strikes independently of the water it interacts with and by its own laws of physics. Once you set eye into that vast empire, no end or alternative seems available. Right where everything seems to adjourn, the clouds mix in colour and dust with the eternity of that mouldy ocean.

At my right, a tiny boat struggling to stay afloat calls me to undertake that uncanny adventure. For a moment, I hesitate, just long enough to feel the rugged touch of that Monster coat chasing me across realities. There is no time for considerations, and suddenly my sight tunnels until all I can see is that sinking boat as the only way forward. I rush to board the decaying raft and I set course towards the unknown.

Time dissipates, as I can no longer measure how long I have been pursuing that monotonous emptiness. The water under me revolves and jumps inside my shell, menacing to extinguish me and everything that I have ever been. The Sun stays pale and disinterested in a static point far away. Night never comes, and

72

the only darkness there is reflected from my wrecked heart.

The uneven wind rumbles the cuirass of the boat with violence, like a guardian removing an unpleasant intruder. The sounds of my memories and everything that I will never have back resounds from the leaky and holey sail, preventing me from finding rest. Twisted in the tiny space that has become my reality, the peace I find is just the cruel reminder of where I will never be again.

I have everything I could ever need right here; yet, there is nothing here that awakens any of my senses or emotions. Just like the water below me, I am dead inside. Because I cannot bury and withhold that sentiment of profound loss here, I know my memories will still torment me should I settle in this world. Because, across the distance, that distasteful and obnoxious Monster is chasing me, claiming its accolade, I must move on... And, as I pronounce that thought, I find myself again on the edge of that desert, ready to start my scouting once more.

Right in front of me, the highest mountain ever conceived stands with an impetuous frailty in it. As the wooden picket bulleted right through my soul sets a constant reminder of the depth of my sorrow, I must not falter now. Redemption only lays staying far away from my pestilent persecutor and stalker; atonement will only be granted if I find a way to maintain the blaze inside of me in plenitude.

Without time for deliberations and scrutiny, I decisively begin the longest hike one could encounter. As I progress towards my ungrateful errand, the rocks I step in vanish unveiling their true nature of fragility. I must tread lightly, as one blunder could shatter and disintegrate this majestic house of cards, entombing me and everything left to fight for with it. I must haste, as the Monster licking my footsteps will not share my delicacy.

I finally reach the peak and climax of that torturous hike. After unbearable hardship and repentance, I am above everything that is earthly and mundane in this reality. I am as high as anyone could ever possibly be. No being in this world could shadow me from where I stand. Yet, as I stop to breath the moment, the rocks below me crack and dust away, shortening that immense and soaring mountain, one inch at the time.

Not even the wind dares to stand as tall as I am now, and the decadent and effete Sun looks up to me with respect. I am so far beyond everything that ever existed that no life has ever defied occurring here. I am the incontestable emperor of this listless and apathetic realm of grime. My only company turns to be the last memoirs of what feeling joy tasted like. They revolt with audacity, scrubbing me that I will never be worthy of them again.

I should feel awe and humbleness and admiration for the sighting of absoluteness in front of me. Yet I feel just emptiness and perplexed nothingness filled with erratic aimless. This is the closest I will ever be to that vast and powerful sky that once belonged to me; yet I am still too far away to reach its grandeur. Moreover, where there was the breath-taking luminous beauty of my Sunset Star, now you will find nothing but a thunderous empty space, colourless and inert. My soul down here is nothing now but a mirror of that emptiness up there.

I have everything I could ever need right here; yet, there is nothing here that awakens any of my senses or emotions. Just like the hollow stones below me, I am dead inside. Because I cannot bury and withhold that sentiment of profound loss here, I know my memories will still torment me should I settle in this world. Because, across the distance, that relentless and dogged Monster is chasing me, claiming its endowment, I must move on... And, as I pronounce that thought, I find myself again on the edge of that desert, ready to give up on my useless crusade once and for all...

While I surrender to the inevitable destiny, I concede that my memories will taunt and torment me no matter how far I seek to hide. The wind then carries that perverted voice again to whack me with the heavy obviousness: "Was it as expected, you dupe?"

And as the words sink in the arid sand around me, my throat recovers its purpose, knowing that I will never be far enough from those memories: "As everything that is beautiful and worthy in this life should never be expected, but born from the inevitable randomness of true caring. Since what haunts me in terror is also a companion that will never leave me no matter how tortuous the path in front of me is. Because no matter how far you stride from everything that you once were, what truly defines you as a being will always be adhered to the walls of your soul. From now on, I aim to expect only the unexpected…"

As everything goes with a sudden quietness around me, a frigid snowflake falls in my forehead. I fall on my knees; it might be the announcement for my final capitulation...

Zdzisław Beksiński. Sanok Museum

<u>PHASE 6</u>: Proclamation

It is dark on this dingy and timeless night. My mind is the reflection of the fastened and dictatorial sky up there. So impetuous, so distinguished, so solemn; yet, so empty and calcaneus, mortified with the weight of everything it has lost. The blood Moon barely casts some light in the pale sand cloak that dominates everything in sight.

I am cloistered in the night that has promised not to end. In the far away distance, I can hear the fireworks announcing the infinite reality of possibilities that is continuously collapsing within every second of existence. However, that joy and elation and ordinariness belong to a truth that my soul is no longer willing to embrace. From where I stand, that feasible existence becomes a chimerical version of me that will never come back.

Closer by, yet out of my apprehension, the Monster meddles waiting for its opportunity to dupe me. Its revolting and tacky smell crumple my nostril with greed. The wind brings and flits its rough and tart hair to remind me there is no place where I can be safe. Moreover, as I am sank into its wearing game, I can even taste its hideous, sordid and vile presence as if that fiend were standing right by my side.

Time bends with the breeze, refusing to elapse in an intuitive way, prolonging every instant of regret and pang. The affliction and bitterness find its way beyond what my cracked soul can endure. I have every reason to start my march in search of friendlier paramos, however I feel unable to move. After roving around all owned and proposed creation, I have finally come to the realisation that it is the time to face the constriction of my long-awaited judgement.

A tiny sparkle appears and jumps arbitrarily around me, with no apparent purpose. The Enchanter has been erected as the prolocutor and mediator to hear and negotiate my final imprisonment. Graceful and delicate she flatters around with impetuous and unpredictable tenderness. This pixie is ready to consider my allegations and offer me the agreement with which I can save my Sunset Star from extinction. Since running is futile, I am ready to comply and affirm the consequences of my happiness.

I know that as long as the negotiations prolong, the last reminiscence of beauty enclosed within *my heart will continue to shine and bring colours; I am aware that while the Enchanter is pricing the extension and gravity of my misery, the Monster must repress its thirst for annihilation. However, I must not forget that the sweet and lithe dance of the nymph is just a trickery of camouflage, as her loyalty belongs to the very same authorities and forces eager to vainglory with my downfall.*

Time has come to set up the price to satisfy such sources of revenge and resentment; time has come to find out how much I will be willing to give in exchange for everything that is good in this world. However, where do you set the bar and the nature of a punishment that brought all sense and purpose to your miserable existence? As my mind asks the question, the Enchanter flies around with nonchalance, expecting more from me.

Since everything that touches my month from now until I grow into the very same dust that cover my feet is just superfluous; as I have no expectancy to ever find anything worthy of the tastes I have experienced in this life; because I don't intend to find anything that will ever satisfy the hunger of my soul. Is my taste and zing an appropriate price to pay for my pride, in exchange for everything that matters? As my mind asks the question, the Enchanter flies around with indifference, demanding more from me. I then lost the gift of taste.

Since I have smelt every tone from the palette of comfort and beauty; as the world is fetid and rotten and mouldered in this decadent reality that I have created; because I don't expect there will ever be any sweetness left for me to discover. Is my scent and pry enough addition to satisfy your sloth and bargain for my redemption? As my mind asks the question, the Enchanter flies around with apathy, awaiting more from me. I then lost the gift of smell.

Since all I can hear now is banal and trivial, without adding any value to my ambitions and expectations; as the sounds that once brought joy and shelter and direction have vanished between my fingers; because everything carried by the wind is made of timeless sorrow, remorse and regret. Is my hearing and heed enough extension to my previous offering in order to calm your anger and save the last light of this world? As my mind asks the question, the Enchanter flies around with disdain, contemplating more from me. I then lost the gift of sound.

Since my touch has lost its way to find the soft velvet that once covered my conscious creation; as now everything feels harsh and ragged like this wooden post meshed to my heart; because anything left to be endured is just fabricated from my own suffering and martyrdom. Is my skin and finesse in conjunction with all the above what will quieten gluttony for retribution? As my mind asks the question, the Enchanter flies around with derision, forecasting more from me. I then lost the gift of touch.

Since my eyes have given up on seeing and seeking for awe anywhere; as I no longer aspire to encounter any new form of worthful grace and artistry ever again; because I was lucky enough to witness closely the source of all inspiration, beginnings and endings in this Universe. Is my sighting and eyes what I need to add up to find gratification in my lust and preserve the pureness left in me? As my mind asks the question, the Enchanter flies around with disparagement, anticipating more from me. I then lost the gift of sight.

Since my mind no longer serves the purposes of my body and existence; as my consciousness has been confused from afar and it's now anchored to a time where I can never return; because my intellect misled me into this aimless and helpless quest that has cost me everything that I conceived. Is my cognition and psyche what is causing such envy and the oblation requested to spare my last wish? As my mind asks the question, the Enchanter flies around with aspersion, assuming more from me. I then lost the gift of awareness.

Since my soul has been shredded into pieces and is ready to crumble and succumb to its fatality; as my heart was torn apart by the very same source that provided it with glow; because the weight of whatever is left to feel is just a painful shadow of everything that lies behind and beyond my reach. Is my spirit and vitality the last remain of greed that I must submit to preserve what is left of my Sunset Star? As my mind asks the question, the Enchanter flies around with calumny, dictating more from me. I then lost the gift of sensitivity.

As I bend down and the sand rushes to cover and enclose as much of me as possible, I am nothing as there is nothing left of me. Yet, the Monster claps and lauds expectant in the background, aware *that it might finally be granted with the forsaken chance to absorb the pieces of my defeat. I ride on the loins of the world I conceived, then witnessed it collapse as a consequence of my pursuit for more.*

Only the Enchanter has stayed by my side during this path towards the deepest dooms of self-destruction and flagellation. And in that mixture between compassion and masochist stalking persecution, my house of cards has finally given up their fragile resistance against the unforgivable grievance. In my final enlightenment, suddenly my turbulent mind peeks what was the failure during all this doomed acumen.

As I finally understand the dispute and obstacle was never rooted in the nature of the answers and requirements; since all this time to what I have failed is not to myself or everything I cared for, but to formulate the right questions. Because I could never expect to obtain the searched solutions for fulfilment and redemption while I still hold down to my corporeal expectations and possessions.

It is now that I realise I was ready to offer only everything that I had and caused torment and pain to my existence. Thus, no sacrifice, but relief I was seeking, the penitence was never meant to amuse and delight my demands. In order to master and enact my ultimate aspiration, I must be ready to pact the retreat of whatever I can find hosting any value in my soul.

It is my memories and love and achievements on everything that brought me joy and meaning the price required of me. Because it is only if I'm ready to face the terror and anguish of letting go on everything I still value and cherish when the bonding bill with this tribunal will be granted. To do that, I must travel to the deepest nooks within my being and trace any remains of happiness and elation to put it up for donation.

As I come to my final realisation and accept the price to pay is everything that I was, am and will be, the light within belonging to my Sunset Star cheer with satisfaction. The sky above opens wide and the Sun comes out of its hiding to witness my ulterior sacrifice. The wind finally stops carrying my pity and memories of better times, and the Enchanter stays in front of me undaunted. To save my beloved beauty, I must annihilate myself.

While I recover all my vain and wasted senses, I gather just enough strength to face the following inevitable step. The wind embraces that immoral and polluted whisper once more showing no mercy to my agony: "Are you ready for it, you patsy?"

And as the words penetrate my wounds and swim through my veins, my recovered guttural voice raises strong into the ruins of my world: "Since I no longer host expectations for redemption; as finally the terms have been dictated, defeating my last hopeless defences; because there is only a final purpose for me to accomplish before all the lights are finally gone. For all I am now is the preserver of truth, I am ready to accept my condemn."

As a majestic sanctuary raises in front of me, standing high and deep where I can no longer foresee, a den opens at its feet welcoming me in. I know

now this will be my final descend. This is the beginning of my end...

Zdzisław Beksiński. Sanok Museum

PHASE 7: Constriction

I kneel with my last inkling of vitality in the blistering sand. With my final punishment dictated, I contemplate the magnificence of an opaque and cragged cave inviting me into my last descend. The residual pieces that once shaped my ego still portrait certain resistance to give in to my only possible destiny. I lay in that burning ground without hope, without reason, without pursue.

The dark red coloured Sun seems morose and dispirited as the judge of this fallen reign. I know I will never be bathed by that impetuous warmth again. The clouds are dispersing in the vast grey sky as their thirst for revenge has been feasted. I know I will never hear their thunderous and envious claims again. The wind no longer carries accusations

and painful images of what will never
return to me. I know I will never taste
that kiss again. As for everything that
being I ever meant, it will vanish the
instant my foot treads into that obscure
and rooted cavern.

However, as I take a breather and
contemplate my faith, I am reminded that
this is no land for hesitation. The
crashing and gelid howl from the
Monster peals across the endless and
arid desert. This demon shows no
intention to accept the covenanted truce.
Like a barbarous executioner, it will
chase me until it can relish with the taste
of my dusty soul and the splendour of my
Sunset Star within.

Possessed by a sudden will for
mobility, I rise like a geyser in the middle
of that sterile waste. I walk and penetrate
into the darkness and isolation from

everything that can be considered the world. Yet, not everything is black. A tiny sparkle clashes in front of me while shimming before my eyes. The Enchanter, once more, tries to divert my attention from the inevitable. However, I have no time for games and amusements, The Monster prowls and the eternal obscurity will not stop it.

I go down a tortuous path that wrings itself with pain and anguish at every turn. Where I am now, I need my senses no more, as there is nothing worth perceiving. The air around me is thick like a bear's fur and it pierces your skin, trespassing every secret corner within your spirit. The ground below feels inhospitable and erratic, making every stride of the way an arduous achievement.

There is nothing to hear in this place, but the distant growl of the barbaric hunter encouraged by the scent of my bloodstream; there are no scents carried in these endless passages, but the noxious and malodorous incense from the stalker and death seeker; the walls are oblate and splay, but broken with the rugged and sour hair left behind by my unflagging chaser; as for everything is drab and gloomy, but the distant red and luminous eyes of the beast reverberate across the sinuous corridors.

As I go deeper and downer in my search for epiphany, the surroundings shrink trying to constrain me and make me an accessory to their cold and meaningless existence. The trail I follow bifurcates over and over again, making each one of the decisions to continue my march a torture of wonder: wonder of where I'm leading myself into, and a wonder of what is it that my choice is leaving behind and I will never find anymore.

I am the furthest away from any other life form as any living being has ever been. Loneliness... trapped with the weight of my nostalgia and the unfulfilled promises for happiness and purposeful goals. With only my vindictive mauler as company inside this self-portrayed prison. As I desperately continue seeking for a heaven of peace where to pay my sentence, all I encounter is desperation and repetitive absurd.

The maze twists and it curls my mind with it, testing the remains of its former glory and strength. My heart, pierced by countless thorns made of memories, is the lucero to guide me on this expedition towards the confines of essence and reality. Every step I take is a realisation that the entire trail covered must hide some sense of sanity at the end. However, I endure this mindless crusade without questioning. The breath of the devil is too close behind my neck for contemplations.

Pathway after pathway, bifurcation after bifurcation, and era after era, I drown deeper, searching for the core and crux that holds the reality continuity. In the real world, this journey started eons ago; in my subjective perception, the time has already collapsed and evaporated between my fingers... Surrender by the dark from where we all raise, now more than ever, the weak light contained and kept within my chest is all that matters.

I finally reach the edge of creation itself. The core where everything is heat and freeze simultaneously. An impetuous and gaunted source of light lying at the bottom of the precipice where all the roads in this grotto find its ending. I now comprehend the origin of the Universe, and I have been deprived of all my senses to host any sensation or reaction in such bearings. As I stand there, I absorb the tragedy: I will never find anyone to share the wisdom I am witnessing.

Where the core and essence to everything that holds a purpose is, only simplicity and pragmatism can be your companion. As for everything that is developed as complex, convoluted and intricate, its foundations are parsimonious and transparent. As I stand before the ultimate enlightening, I learn with awe that behind every colossal, abstract and hefty question ever made, a pure and effortless answer is awaiting to be acknowledged.

Tears. Tears of desperation and apprehension fall down my cracked skin and into the core of revelations that rests at my feet in this magnificent pit. Tears that amalgamate themselves where all the riddles are solved with simplicity. Where I stand right now, I comprehend that the futilities and individualities of our existence do not matter; that I am not a consequence of the space and time continuum that I once mastered, but we are all a unity with everything that exists, as otherwise nothing could ever have been conceded.

I am the mandatory observer to give way and meaning to the conception and establishment of everything that was, is and will be. The heat invades me through every pore of my wasted crust. For a very brief instance, I recall what it was like to feel the will to continue living. Finally, I will never experience the need for any further questions, since I discovered that all the answers where within and not to be searched in the convulsed world. It is not happiness, but only emptiness and incredulity awaiting you at the end of that rainbow where all answers are found: it is the gift of awareness and insight the rewards you obtain.

The wisdom I am being gifted with is yet too great to be fully assimilated. The implications of it overflows my intellect. I now know the trail to follow spontaneously, as hesitation stays trapped by that pit. Right at the end of the darkest path, I will find the room for reflection and reconsideration.

As I walk those last steps of my journey, a silent space is exposed, leading to a chamber less leeway. For all I know, the Monster will never find the correct way to track me here. Stepping in, the walls around become generous and spacious once more, and the stones impaling them reflect a non-existent light source. The ceiling is curved and recycles the air with exhilaration. Right at the end, a magnanimous mirror, engraved from the floor and encrusted all the way up to the ceiling, overshadow everything else.

As I stand in front of it, nothing is reflected back at me. No trace of my being or corporality that I once cherished and hosted with impetus. Just blackness bended with the rest of the room, and the shiniest of blazes right where my heart should be: the legacy entrusted by my Sunset Star endures now that soon must be released. Because life is filled with irony and whimsy by giving me all the answers when I can no longer make use of them.

While I inhale my quietude in the middle of that chamber, my mind rests assured everything is closing down to a deserved ending. Yet, a soft breeze finds its way to my consciousness to torment me once more: "Did you understand it, you lackey?"

And, as I regained my forgotten vulnerability, I find the only empty and blanc points in my reality: "As I have found the answer to all the questions ever made, I also gathered the ultimate purpose for existence itself. For everything we fight to construct and identify us with is just the back of a hollow mirror where we all end up going through. Yet, the ultimate realisation is the one which you will never be aware of; because I acknowledge my supreme ignorance when I know the most, I understood it."

And, as those words crave and dig sharply through every particle of reality, suddenly the last tiny piece resisting the awaken of proficiency becomes bigger than every other wisdom combined. It is then when my mind encounters agitation and anguish where placid harmony should be resting...

Zdzisław Beksiński. Sanok Museum

PHASE 8: Presagement

As I stand in the middle of absolute solitude, the sparks coming from the wall can barely fight with the dense darkness reigning. I am surrounded by cavities that lead to any new corner of this puzzling collection of galleries. Yet, I choose to stay still in the centre of this majestic, craggy and mournful hall where an empty mirror patrols every single one of my shallow breaths. The concave ceiling occasionally drops blobs filled with sand and paraffin.

There is no more remorse, emptiness, craving or will emanating. So little is left of what I once stood for, that even the mirror that accompanies me does not appreciate the worth of reflecting me. Silence. Terrifying silence broken only by the pulse of my moribund and erratic heart. Every capricious beat that decides to fade and go missing feels like a merciful break.

No signs of what the world must be like out of this cave; no signals from the past, present or future; no warnings indicating whether I am still alive or if this dark place will host my soul for eternity; no stimuli hinting at the whereabouts of the Monster or the Enchanter. Just absolute isolation to discover that the opposite of positiveness is not negativeness, but nothingness.

Then, all the possibilities presented as holes and trails leading to all directions collapse before me. Suddenly, there is no way out of this room even if I wanted to. It becomes clear that this space will premiere the ballet performance of my own requiem. My mind, once capable of crafting all the beauty and greatness with a stroke of my hand, is now the architect of this perfectly designed confinement for my soul, body and existence.

Then, when everything is dark, silent, colourless and ending, I feel the last gleam of heat coming from my chest. Where my heart used to settle whole and meaningful, the remains of my Sunset Star still collide to shine amongst dust and sorrow. An immense urge for insurrection erupts from the very essence of my being, denying the reality of my fate. The refusal for this ending invades the room with light and luminosity, and every corner of the room becomes movement, rebellion and turmoil abruptly.

"I repudiate my destiny as it is being driven to its final call, thus I stand tall acknowledging there is still a world filled with alternatives waiting to be conquered." - *I claim out loud, reverberating from wall to wall and breaking the thick fog of gloom that prevailing my tomb. Finally, my crying finds its way into that deep, acute and devious mirror, abandoning this reality. As I resurface with renewed motives and intent, I find no answer nor repercussion in return.*

Then, when everything is dark, silent, colourless and ending, I feel the uncontainable ignition of the conflagration and purifying blaze. And every single predicament of that cage is challenged with the rage and anger of awareness. The very same foundations that sustain that unbreakable and invisible cavern crumble and hesitate. My exasperation ascends like a tyrannical emperor, ready to knuckle and demolish this denouement.

"I brawl against giving up the very same birr that once dominated, sculpted and construed the layouts hiding under all the mundane appearances." - *I wailed breaking through the blue flares with the animosity and blinded determination of an uncontainable blast. I swing and strike in the sturdy walls where all the possible grottos used to offer me alternatives. As my enmity and exasperation grow empty inside that silent mirror, I find no answer nor repercussion in return.*

Then, when the flames start to consume and extinguish, consequence of their own mindless obsession, quietness emerges once more. I need to come to terms where I am able to reconcile the reality that is being pushed down my throat and my eagerness for redemption.

I am ready to accept any penitence that will allow me just one more opportunity to master all the power that was entrusted in me. My willingness to find an accord transpires through every pore and rift within the walls that imprison my future.

"Name a price that will leave me just enough of myself to protect and endure everything I ever dreamed of. Take everything you see fit, but the component of me that thrives for real connection." - *I implored down my knees, searching for a counteroffer that might allow me to save my uniqueness. I erect myself naked in body and soul, rebuffing and withdrawing what I foolishly believed that made my existence real. As I stare at that judgmental and frivolous mirror, I find no answer nor repercussion in return.*

Then, when all my means and skills have been vanquished, I find myself in the deepest of hardships and repentances. I disintegrate into an essence that only transpires grief and deprivation. As I become part of the blackness that rules this catacomb, the phantom of depression takes its chance to cover me with heavy layers of sorrow and unfulfilled promises. I have achieved nothing with all the gifts I was granted with; therefore, I pay the price for my ultimate and fatal failure.

"I have wasted and rotten all the beauty and allure I was awarded with. I will never find a recovery from all the self-sabotage I have endured myself into. I degraded all the colours, covering them with a dense and impermeable coating of dilapidation" - *I mutilate myself as the sole perpetrator of my own misfortune. I annihilate whatever desire for resolution*

I once hosted. As I dissolve everything that made me feel worthwhile in front of the reflectionless mirror, I find no answer nor repercussion in return.

Then, a deafening feel of peace and balance embraces my mind. As I rebuild and come to terms with my flaws and defects, I accept that every step of this suicidal journey has led me exactly to the planned completion. Because I was never designed to shape the contortions of this reality, yet I enjoyed and dared with the idea of unveiling every single riddle standing in front of me. I witnessed the whole palette and scope offered: from absolute obscurity until the brightest revelations, and my soul were broken and dissolved in life as a result.

"I am ready to welcome that gentle good night and the everlasting price for everything that I have been. Yet, I accept what I cannot change anymore and embrace what endured and defeated my resilient soul until this last breath" - *I resurge from the ruins of my own life and set my spirit into the next phase of this never-ending journey. As I endeavour with a solemn gratitude that the sunlight will never clasps my skin again and get ready to find myself on the other side of the blurry mirror, I find no answer nor repercussion in return.*

There is no valid deniability, fury, bargaining, abjection or admission that will counter what has been sacrificed and lost for this quest. The cavern that hosts me now is too far gone and away from any source of light. Sometimes you get broken in places and ways that cannot be fixed or amended. In occasions you must be ready to pay a price that is above its value, yet it is worth it.

My vision was blurred and obfuscated by the weight and promise of escaping my own destiny. I dared to break the rules of nature by unveiling its mysteries, yet I obliterated that a scale always seeks for balance: when one side of it over floods with hope and achievement, the opposite pole of the substantial continuum is filled with sorrow and anguish. I found so many answers that the calibration collapsed on both extremes before I was able to unravel the true essence of existence. I was so fixated shaping every hidden cranny of concreteness and corporeality that I never learnt how to transcend my creation through intuitive connection.

The very same core of my being and universal energy is corrupted, and it should no longer return to the stream and current of eternity and integrity. It is now, on the dawn of a New Day for desire and cherish, when I must walk down the path of looseness until I am dissolute with matter and not with spirituality. It is there how the river will continue to flow and every drop of discovery, loss, sorrow, amusement, evolution, anguish and awe onto everything that will occur after I cease to occur.

It is now that I finally glimpse the final descent of this journey, when my individuality and plurality are ready to extinguish. It is in this secret and curved cavern, where no one will never find me, where the transformation and revolution of reality will begin. As I lie down ready to melt into the rocky ground, that mocking voice catches up on me with defiance: "Will you remember it, you gull?"

And as I master and gather in the palm of my hand everything that I was, perceived and created, I comply: "As I have agreed to lose everything that is corporeal and materialistic; as I will have to give up my soul and everything that is eternal too; since my biggest failure lays in the impossibility to eclipse my own temporal existence, every memory is a breath for unfulfilled hope and a reminder to everlasting and rise above your capabilities. Because this light deserves sharing, I will not remember, nor follow the natural path into the after-life; yet, everyone else will remember everything."

And, as I admire that questioning and vacant mirror, a sudden crack in the wall severs a piece of gravel, spitted from its very luminous core. It is the Engraving

Stone, giving purpose to my decided and dying last breaths...

Zdzisław Beksiński. Sanok Museum

PHASE 9: Expurgation

I stand in the middle of this empty room. No way out, no source of light. The sparkles dripping from within the walls are dusty and quiet now: they have lost their particularity and imposition. The ceiling is curved and high, yet it pushes away the limited air available to breath. What once was my eternal dawn of lightness is now a moribund excuse to believe there is still something left of my Sunset Star in this world. And that mirror… that ardent and fervid mirror observes me with contempt and an impasible chasm that ignores my own reflect.

On my feet lays the Engraving Stone with which I must ensure all this brainless journey lingers in harmony and tranquillity. Because nothing is truly perished while it still finds connection within this world, and the brightness that captivated me and sealed my fate must prevail when the New Day comes. Yet what truly penetrates and punctures your soul cannot be shared with common words.

Now that my last strands of holy energy decay and whiter in this lonely nook, it is when I must produce my most magnanimous creation: the one that will seal my legacy. It is now, with my last exhalations, when I uncover the sarcastic and sardonic truth: that our outvie as beings is not to flourish from beauty, success and triumph; but it regurgitates from the grime and dredge of our countless failures and the struggle to perpetuate.

As I must render and transcribe this never-ending story about the essence of *the spirit, no words materialise in my mind to be executed by my hand. Hesitation is seeded from the simplicity required to expound the most basic and convoluted principle that there is. Sometimes you cannot make justice by any means of expression if the feeling is pure. And there is nothing more authentic and unadulterated than thriving following the instinct of the soul in pursuit of ultimate brightness.*

Thunderous coups rumble abruptly from the other side of the reverberating wall. The growls and yowls leave no room for ambiguity: the Monster is pressing to come in and conclude the circle of persecution. I can smell its mephitic and reeking presence, touch its grating and rasping fur, and my mind shivers with the sound of its desperate screaming. Everything arrives heighten and magnified on this side of the divider. My time of consciousness, as the time to decipher everything that is delightful, is slipping through my fingers...

Fear will paralyse me no more, nor will I flee from my fate this time. This is the moment and time when I have the chance to define how I will be remembered in the world I leave behind. When the beast finds its way through into my reality, I will wait with the placidity and composure of a serenaded lake in the middle of a quiet night. The satisfaction of my life's oeuvre finished will trespass the barriers that held me prisoner in this world and make me boundless, like my Sunset Star.

The booming smacks taste like music announcing the cease of this endless war transpiring closer and closer. One more titanic quest and, then, my infinite and timeless rest. There are no more questions, no more crying for reparation, no trace of wonder and grandeur. Just one magnanimous story to provide with connotation and nuance every shade of grey and obscurity ruling this world.

I grab the Engraving Stone with the determination of whom has nothing to lose, since everything has already been lost; with the conviction of whom understands that, in order to lose everything, firstly you must have been gifted with everything in return. As my hand grips tightly around this crafting and perpetual rock, my whole existence flashes right in front of my eyes. I summarise every grasps of air and life consumed ever since my eyes where nothing but closeness. The story that must be imprinted for eternity comes clear as a breeze of revelation.

Just before delineating the first image, a luminous spark floats by my side: The Enchanter, for whom the limitations of space and time are irrelevant, caught up with me once more to escort me during my final task. Perhaps this nymph seeks to be the beacon that will guide the Monster towards me, perhaps its hunger for mocking me craves to see my fatal descend. It matters no more, as all that is left to be important again is to craft my audacity and hike towards resurgence and immaculate beauty.

I carve and ingrain the lines that represent all the truths of my life in the shape of drawings. Each illustration reveal a step towards my downfall, and the necessity of all the anguish and pain. Soon my hands are brisker than the incise penetrating the stones, and with each slit and cleavage, a new colour is discovered behind the superfluous layer. Slowly my solitude is filled with glow and pigments that fight and cover the strikes in the shaking wall on the edge of collapse.

For each mark, the Enchanter remains by my side, observing with admiring awe and laceration. Like a muse, she whispers me the inspiration to drive the next twist of my wrist. Under her light, I experience warmth and connection in a sensation I believed to be prohibited to me. Her calm and support provide me with the energy I require to continue, one breath at a time, into translating the shapes of existence.

Moreover, each mark engraved finds an exact reflection on the inside surface of my soul; with each drawing my spirit bleeds and agonise in pain and torment. Invisible to the naked eye, the fatal and necessary wounds mirror all the anguish endorsed to reach this point. Because in life it is what we cannot see what ends up killing you. But I cannot cease in my mission, the story must be perpetuated for eternity; the misery and affliction soon will find its completion in the hands of my unsparing and fusty persecutor, screeching closer and closer through that wall.

As the graphics and sketch enrich their shape and learn their meaning and representation, a ghost projects itself from each one of the represented occurrences. Thick, translucid, shomber phantoms that mimic the very same events that drove me to this merciless conclusion. Soon the room is filled with memory spectres that dance and torture me in this grotesque carnival. They flutter *with the weight that their essence and connotation has over my decaying soul.*

Fixation on the ongoing task becomes sordid and defying, surrender by images and reminders of everything that I loved and lost; by the uproarious noise that will consume and shatter my last holding point to life when the barrier vanishes; by that silent and pedantic mirror that refuses to project what's left of me with disgust; by the physical agony emerging from each cell of my corporeality, which is only the shadow of the spiritual bitterness that wrings my inside, breaking it memory by memory.

Yet, the Enchanter lingers by my side with her gracile movement and her azure observation and support. It is because of her that I find new ways to contort my hands in new methods that brings to life more of those haunting memoirs. It is now, when the road is almost at its consummation, when I feel the alleviation and exhilaration of spiritual connection one last time. This brief moment with the Enchanter, from whom I have been hiding all along, becomes the last breeze of positivity that will cross my pierced existence.

It is almost done; the fairy-tale has been dreamt, lived, collapsed, destroyed and forecasted for eternity inside this room of atonement. It is time to summarise everything that was ever worth a feeling. My hands are filled with blisters; my soul crumbles and can no longer endeavour the emotional pain that has been bearing since before the world disintegrated. It is now that my mission has been completed. I might not have been able to preserve my consciousness and wholeness, but I was only conceived as the vehicle of courage and sustainment for the eternal allure of the spherical creation in this universe.

As I delineate the closing depiction that narrates the epos towards significance, all the ghosts stop and stay still with anticipation. Even the noise and the strikes cease. The hollow mirror turns deep black and closes. Suddenly, everything is quiet and contemplative. The final time is upon me. As I stand in the centre of permanence, that spoofing and outwit voice softly whispers, standing right behind my ear: "Are you ready, you twerp?"

And as I try to gather the remains of my bravery to turn around and face what was the traced plan all along, I accord: "As I have lived enough to master all the purposes and answers of life, and lost them all; since I have completed the only task I was created for; because everything from here would be superfluous and filled with melancholic memories. I am ready for the fatal expiation."

And as I embrace my last words, all the shadows abandon me and burst into dust; all the colours and scents of this world bloom from the indents I crafted in the walls; the mirror becomes transparent and honest as a virgin and quiet lagoon; and the wall behind me explodes sliding a blinding light that only gives away the silhouette of my executioner. It is now that I am perishing, when I can see everything that represents truth for the first time...

Zdzisław Beksiński. Sanok Museum

PHASE 10: Resurgence

The blinding warm light penetrates through my eyelids, driving a feeling of unstoppable relief across my veins. Suddenly, the space and matter that confine my body shrinks to contain the continuous dripping of my exhausted and corrupted energy. Finally, my eyes open. In front of me, the walls of this cavern pounce on me. For an impetuous moment, the external light, yellow and fatigued, collapses my senses until all the colours of reality run away one by one.

I stand on my knees, with my arms opened, waiting for the final strike; but nothing happens. I close my eyes and lift my head, tasting the sweetness of nostalgia one last time; but nothing happens. I accept the journey that have sealed my fate, expecting the last of lights to be turned off; but nothing happens. I harbour the inner contentment of having depicted and rendered the preservation of everything ever considered as graceful for the last time; but nothing happens.

I can foresee the contour of that Monster that has stalked me since my ascension through the blinding light in the open cavity; yet it resides motionless. I can scent the revolting odour coming from that brute that has been haunting me restlessly; yet it resides motionless. I can sense the thick and bawdy pelage that covers the ogre with an endless thirst to fulminate the last spark of light and hope; yet it resides motionless. I can feel the desire of annihilation and decimation in the soul of that troll rejoicing the seizure of his long awaited prey; yet it resides motionless.

I have conquered the tallest of mountains, found my course through the leafiest of forests, endeavoured the wildest of the storms, traversed through the barrenest of deserts... All with the clearest of purposes; all for the wrongest of reasons. Yet it is now that I have harvested the real price and resolution of my pilgrimage, when I stand still deluged in confusion. It is now, that I am ready to relish my fatal condemnation, embracing the destiny I have absconded in the claws of my executioner, when the corporality of the world finally freezes.

My legs are raised by bewilderment and turmoil, seeking to unmask the truthiness avoiding to be acknowledged and standing in front of me. I recall every inch of the etching with my fingertips, looking to interpret that final answer. Each wall and each colour emanated from them tell a fulfilling story that does not leave any room for further interpretations or endings. However, as I complete my scouring without success, I suddenly comprehend there is yet one part of my odyssey that remains unexplored: that hushed and glistering mirror that oversees time, space and reality.

I cluster and endure my fortitude to be judged one last time: however, this time I will perpetuate my own decree. Where the soul stands naked, nothing provided from the corporeal world or from your mental reassurance can shelter you in front of the Mirror of Acumen. Finally, one last chance to exalt myself with the portrayal of the last remaining of my Sunset Start. My final connection with the grandeur I once hosted.

I stand tall and determined in front of that Mirror of Acumen. Then, my whole perception collapses and shatters into dust, contemplating the mere and hard reality displayed to me this whole time. Suddenly, every piece of self-reflection and achievement falls apart, crashed by the weight of the evidence that I chose to neglect. Finally, I discern my willingness to truly glimpse my plot in this sadistic spectacle.

As I contemplate myself in front of that fount of clarity, tears run wild and down my seamed face. It is not eyes what allow my vision, but two haunting red beams; it is not a smile what my mouth draws, but a jaw with endless and piercing teeth; it is not skin what covers my body and spirit, but a dense, gruff and ribald pelt; it is not in hands where my arms end, but in fierce and sharpened claws; it not the smell of a meaningful creation what I see, but the putrid stench bloomed from the rotten; as it is not what myself used to be what the Mirror of Acumen rebounds, but that very same Monster from whom I was negating all along.

I portrayed myself as the solemn hero long enough to become the atrocity of this world. I was so blinded by my own pursuit that I ignored my own descend into the hell of vanity and corruption. I became the toxic pattern which I swore to protect my Sunset Star from. I was so consumed with my quest that I did not allow myself to breathe the nature laying at plain sight. I searched in the entire world of existence for answers that sojourned within me right from the start...

I crumble and burst in despair, crunched by my own realisation and awakening. I curse and darn my fate and path, adulterating and polluting everything that ever held any beauty within. I am the puppet sustained by the rotten strings that I fabricated. I am the only blaming source for all that was wrongful and wrecking my cherish and joy. As for all that chasing and running, I was only postponing my own enlightenment and confrontation with my flaws and demonization.

As I condemn myself in the ground, a warm stroke in my shoulder lifts my aura. I raise my head with wonder to discover that silhouette by the door has approached me, witnessing my spiritual demolition. In my moment of most need, during my darkest night, this eternal light finds compassion and repentance within the pieces of my heart. As I sense the eternal gift of forgiveness, I understand my walk of atonement is yet inconclusive.

It was not a fierce beast, but my all allured Sunset Star the one that chased me across my own maze relentlessly. It was her the one that never gave up on me, even when I did; it was her the one who persisted in escorting me through my deepest passage; it was I whom consciously ran away from everything that I ever yearned for. It is in this moment of reunion, when contrition consolidates all the faults and blunders that drove my own downfall into the catacombs of my self-created purgatory.

As I connect with my Sunset Star, seeking for compassion and clemency, it is then when I observe she is not whole and complete. There, in her chest, a missing segment is filled with obscurity *instead of brightness; here, where my heart was, lays the piece with the exact matching shape to complete her. I thought I was benefiting the very same source of my own pureness, yet I teared and usurped what was holy and immaculate to me. In the name of love, I portrayed the largest of cruelties ever conceived.*

I subtract the last part of myself that deserves my love and admiration, assuming that it will request my consciousness in exchange. As I tear apart the last blaze of light in me, my perception is filled with coldness, dejection and a renewed mystification of equilibrium. I hand over the oblation with humbleness, expecting my imminent self-destruction. My Sunset Star takes my offering gracefully, finding completeness and eternal refinement once again.

Once more, the colours of creation find their place into reality one by one. In my final agony, the Enchanter sparks and flutters, guiding me towards that overture that conduct to the unbearable brightness. It is one last ascension before the long scouted and everlasting lean. Encouraged by my persistent nymph, I now envision her true motives: to support and guard me steadfastly, while I was lost and sightless to reason and reality.

I walk out of that temple of torment, leaving behind everything that I fabricated to demolish myself. Where I am going now, I will require no weight from everything that fed the core of my essence. Belatedly, the time to disburse for my audacity has caught upon me. It is now that I must bequeath, whatever contoured, every shard that once pertain me as a being. As where the soul succumbs, connection and attachment stays behind, welded to everything you loved and loved you in return.

As I look around, I am once more in that endless field, guarded by the transparent blue sky, the joyful clouds, and the luminous Sun. And all the elements welcome me with joy and amusement where I wrongly interpreted judgment and prejudice. It is now that I realise I was my very own accuser, judge, witness and jury all along. The circle is closed: everything ends right where it started.

I lay down in that mud that welcomed me during my fall. As I grasp it with my fingers, flowers and grass gloom and sprout, covering my decrepit corpse with colour and life. As I glimpse the last time I will ever see at all, I find my Sunset Star reborn up there, in that eternal and *unreachable sky. It shows herself whole, radiant, brilliant, magnificent and glorious: she is now the Dawn Star, reborn from my own calamity, brighter than ever. We both have found our rightful places at a distance that will separate us for eternity. Yet, observing her from that prohibitive distance, I know she hosts everything that was ever worth within me; I know whatever is left of me after I perish, it will be retained in her.*

For the last time, as my eyes vanish and my soul comes back to the soil from where it once flourished, my old friend the timing wind brings me his last whisper: "was it worth it, you candid?"

As my senses cease one after the other, I raise my voice for the last time to respond to the demands of this corporeal life companion, the time: "you can only find the source of true happiness and meaning through the same trail of pain and sorrow; for everything that hurts, there is an echo of delight far stronger and lasting. Because everything that transcends in us is tied up to the raw emotions that drive our existence. Since I have endeavoured all the scales of sorrow and anguish, I have witnessed and experienced all the colours and bliss ever conceived. Because denying your pain means surrender your benediction. As it only required giving up every pinch of my soul and consciousness, it was worth it…"

And, just like that, I ceased to exist. Just like that, I re-joined the eternal flow of the Quantum Self…

BE PART OF THE JOURNEY DISCOVERING QUANTUM PSYCHOLOGY!

- **Stay tuned:**

TheInvisibleBookOfQuantumPsychology.com

Facebook.com/SMQuantumPsychology/

Instagram.com/the.invisible.book.of.qp/

Twitter.com/SM68847232

- **Books coming soon:**

☛ Quantum Psychology:

Re-Thinking Time, Space and

Interpersonal Connections

☛ The Invisible Book of Quantum

Psychology

E-book, paper book and audio book available

for pre-order on Amazon

Printed in Great Britain
by Amazon